This is an Em Querido book
Published by Levine Querido

LQ
LEVINE QUERIDO

www.levinequerido.com · info@levinequerido.com
Levine Querido is distributed by Chronicle Books, LLC
Originally published in México in 2022 as **Códice peregrino** by Fondo de Cultura Económica
Text copyright © 2022 by Vivian Mansour
Illustrations copyright © 2022 by Emmanuel Valtierra
English translation copyright © 2025 by Carlos Rodríguez Cortez
All rights reserved
Library of Congress Control Number: 2024942372
ISBN 9781646145157
Printed and bound in China

Published in February 2025
First Printing

Book design by Semadar Megged
The text type was set in Raleigh LT Std.

The illustrations were first drawn by Emmanuel Valtierra by hand on paper, then scanned and digitized into Photoshop and painted with a limited palette, to evoke the old codices. The most important influence on his work is the Boturini Codex, but in general his lines and aesthetics are closer to the Mixtec Codices.

PILGRIM CODEX

Vivian Mansour ◦ **Emmanuel Valtierra** ◦ **Carlos Rodríguez Cortez**

Levine Querido

MONTCLAIR • AMSTERDAM • HOBOKEN

We, the Vargas Ramírez family, come from a faraway place north of Tenochtitlán called Iztapalapa, Land of Clay Upon Water.

A land surrounded by cars and dry grass. A place where the pieces of our small world were scattered.

For some time, we lived there.

On the other side of the plaza, a hill soared. Within the hill, there was a church where we went to offer roses to the Virgen de Guadalupe.

One day, my dad heard a bird's song, a beautiful song that rose up and appeared to say *tihui, tihui, tihui: let's go, let's go, let's go*.

Now we call that mountain The Place of the Prompt Exit.

So we gathered our friends who made up that small world. There were seven people:

Amaranta, Turquoise Mosaic, my father's sister, who carried a baby in her stomach; Reyes, The Archer, Rubén's friend, who knows a messenger; Rubén, Xochimilca, The One with the Silent Smile; Joaquín, my dad, The Warrior of the Taxis; Citlali, my mom, The Princess of the Neighborhood; and Justo, my cousin, The Tlatoani of the Gym.

When we passed by Coyoacán, we were spotted by residents of the area who asked us:

"Where are you going?"

"To the other side."

"Let us join you."

Like this, Eusebio—The Yamerito—and David—The One with the Sacred Tattoo—joined the group. We all left that same month: 1 Flint.

We walked and took bus after bus until we arrived at Guanajuato, Land of the Frogs. We settled afoot a tree so grandiose that five men circling it, side-by-side, could not wrap themselves around it.

We took out our itacates: omelets and tamales. We were going to start eating when suddenly the dark shadow of the tree we sat under was colored in by a swarm of white butterflies. We stopped eating.

My father said, "It's a good omen."

"How will we know that we've arrived to the other side?" I asked. "Will we have to look for another sign?"

"Yes, we'll know we've arrived when we see a feathered man flying over metallic trees."

We walked and we walked and we walked. We arrived at a hotel. There, we waited three days. One abrupt afternoon, some figures known as the Gunmen appeared.

These were the Tiras, Solar Evils.

Fear held on to my mind like a monkey.

We fled through the fire escape. There, a van was waiting for us. Only eight of us entered. One on top of the other, hunched, in between the spaces of the seats.

"And the others?" I asked softly. I had Justo's elbow close to my mouth.

"They're the first sacrifices," he whispered.

The van was running. It was an enraged jaguar.

"Will there be more sacrifices?" I asked, shaking.

"I don't know. But from here on," my father proclaimed, "we are not what we were: now we are Migrant Warriors."

"Shut up!" ordered the driver.

I shut up. I slept. The night absorbed me.

The van stopped abruptly. The driver screamed, "Get off! Quick!"

He threw us out on the road, to a darkness as dense as an obsidian forest.

We all stopped, bewildered. Then a new voice splattered the dark: "Time to walk."

We didn't ask anything. We walked. And walked and walked.

Time continued its march.

All of a sudden, it wasn't just us anymore; there were more people in our procession. A man, a woman, and a child younger than me. I couldn't make them out very well, because the black consumed everything, but there they were, with us, walking in silence.

I could hear a *chic-chac* in the middle of what seemed like a forest. What beings were following us?

"Don't fall behind!" ordered my dad with fear in his voice. "There are coyotes. And they're waiting for us to grow tired."

There were no lights, no lanterns, no cell phones. I barely made out Dad's silhouette, since they'd told us to only wear black clothing.

One of the women exclaimed, "My feet are killing me. My shoes are torn up."

We came to a halt.

"Wait one moment," the guiding voice ordered.

My mom offered me a cracker while we rested. We had only eaten canned tuna, corn kernels, and crackers. Scarce amounts of water, only sips from the jug Dad was carrying.

Someone was crying: it was the woman whose feet ached. Mine didn't hurt, but they beat like a heart trapped inside tennis shoes.

We slept on the grass that night, without knowing exactly where we lay. There were no lullabies nor anyone to rock us to sleep, only the howls of coyotes.

I saw in the distance, very close to the sky, fistfuls of lights with the shine and color of caramels.

I wanted to find the constellations I'd learned about in school.

But after a while, I realized they weren't stars: they were the few lights of a city, of the world sleeping on the other side.

How's the other side? Are they taller? Is everyone rich? What do burgers taste like over there? Does every house have a pool? Are they all white? Do they all use perfume? Does everyone wear rings? Will we be rich over there? Will Mom be in the beauty salon every day? Will Dad buy name-brand clothes and throw them away after one time wearing? Will I be able to fix my teeth and get rid of this horrible metal one I have? It was with these thoughts I fell asleep.

Light scooped out the haunting darkness. We were in a dry forest, ambushed by prickly cactus and animal poops.

The guide, who had been camouflaged by the darkness all night, let himself be seen. He was very young, almost as much as Justo. But my cousin's eyes only knew weights and gym mirrors. The coyote's eyes were nebulous and sly.

He took out his cell phone and asked someone for shoes for the young woman. I was surprised they could communicate with each other.

"You are going to have to carry her for a few hours," he said, looking intently at the men.

She was on the floor, crying, her feet covered in sores and blisters like little red erupting volcanoes. Eusebio and Justo took turns carrying her. That made us walk slower.

We tied another set of days together.

We stopped at a place with a hill. I christened it as The Place Where Feet Cry.

Something good happened on 10 Flint: a dog appeared. Spotted like a jaguar, but skinny like sugarcane. A stray dog, creole, abandoned. I'd take a step and he'd follow. If I stopped, he'd stop.

"Shooo! Go away." The guide tried to scare him off.

"No. He can help us fend off the coyotes," I pointed out.

"And accompany us in the underworld," the guide added, somberly. But he didn't shoo him away anymore.

Observing the dog's and my hair carefully, I realized we both had small white locks of hair on our heads.

He's your aluxe, I heard my Yucatec grandmother's cascading voice in my head.

We ate canned tuna. And only three sips of water each.

Night again, walk in the darkness, ears open like eyes. A scream. Someone fell into a ditch. Eusebio's voice. They rescued him in the dark.

"He's got a broken arm."

"We're gonna leave you here," said the coyote.

"No. It's my third time trying to get to the other side. I've already tried crossing on The Bestia."

"The Bestia?" I asked.

"It's a train, but it has jaws that can eat off one of your arms or legs. They sent me back to Honduras on the Bus of Tears after. I have to do it this time. Help me. I don't want to be The Yamerito anymore."

He sobbed. His story left us scared. My mom wrapped his arm with a T-shirt.

Thirst. A lizard in my throat. I dreamt of a pitcher filled with pineapple juice and lots of ice.

Then, time changed paths . . .

Again, walk in the darkness. The day introduced itself to the night. On day 13 Flint, we arrived at the Río Bravo, Place Where the Waters Tangle.

"Can all of you swim?" the coyote asked.

I knew how, but my dad had warned me beforehand to say I didn't.

"No. No. No," each one said.

"Then get undressed. Keep your underwear on. And put your clothes in black bags. You'll use them as a float."

My mom squeezed my hand. She didn't want to take off her clothes.

"Oh, sir," my dad begged, "have mercy on my wife and allow her to keep something on."

"I don't want to, so that's how she'll go," declared the Elder Coyote.

My mom lowered her head and undressed. Amaranta, with her belly, also undressed.

"Are we there yet, Dad?" I asked again.

"I said no!" Dad got mad at me. But I didn't have the energy to cry.

My aluxe looked at me with saddened eyes. He didn't want to cross the river. I petted him and whispered, "We'll see each other again, but not in the underworld."

The dog licked my hand. A pact between friends.

A whistle was heard in the middle of the night. It was a sign.

From the darkness, thirty other people and another coyote, younger than ours, emerged.

The Younger Coyote had a massive trailer wheel. He offered it to ours, the Elder Coyote.

The Younger Coyote dived into the river with the tire tied to a rope that didn't seem too thick. He disappeared in the waters, taking the rope. I assumed he swam to the other side.

The Elder Coyote told us:

"Grab onto the tire and your plastic bags. Help each other out with your legs."

In an instant, everyone was in the water and had grabbed on to a piece of the tire. Except the man with the broken arm and us.

The coyote questioned, "And you all?"

"We'll wait for the next go-around," Dad responded.

"Don't be stupid. There is no next time." And so we had to enter the river. My breath escaped me upon feeling the freezing cold of the water. In the darkness, it was like throwing yourself into a hole full of ice.

My dad forced the others to leave us a piece of the tire. There were so many of us that we couldn't fit! He grabbed on to Justo's leg.

"Grab on tight, please. Do not let go, no matter what."

I had never heard him speak in that tone before.

The man with the broken arm grabbed on to someone else's leg.

Then, the person on the other side began to pull the tire. There were water currents that licked our legs: marine monsters that wanted to drag us to the bottom.

You could hear the roar of the helicopters over the river. They lifted waves.

We arrived on the other side, frozen and scared to death.

Getting out, drenched, I asked Dad, "Are we there yet?"

"No, not yet. But we're close."

We took off our wet underwear and put on the clothes we had stored in the bags.

Once again, time to walk.

We stopped one night. Amaranta took out a little photo of the Virgen de Guadalupe. We all prayed. Even the guide. I felt the image illuminate the darkness.

"There are snakes that come out at night," warned the coyote. "It's a good thing we have a pregnant woman."

"Why?" asked Mom, worried.

"They say if you travel with a pregnant woman, all the snakes that cross your path will be asleep."

We looked at Amaranta as if she were a divine amulet.

Aside from snakes, there was another enemy: cactus spines that penetrated tennis shoes like swords. And the thirst. There wasn't any more water in the jug. We had to drink water from puddles.

"Lime or horchata?" Reyes quipped. There's always a comedian. And I did laugh. It had been a while.

A metal sheet house appears.

"Watch your belongings," Mom warned.

"What stuff? We have nothing. Only clothes."

But clothes and shoes are valuable.

The house was filled with people who were waiting for the signal and money to cross. Many good people and many bad people.

We all slept together. Dad and me on one end and Mom always close to us, with fear in her eyes. The gazes of the bad people upon her body were as dangerous as the spines of the cacti from our journey.

When I woke up, I found my shoes had been stolen.

Dad grabbed me by my arms and shook me angrily and had to give me his shoes. They fit me big. He ended up barefoot.

The coyote screamed at us that it was time to go. We ran out of the house and followed him. And we walked and we walked. From one moment to the other, we were no longer in a forest, but on a road.

The patrols howled like wolves, hungry for us. They wanted Mexica prisoners to dismember our dreams and send them to the Evil King of the Other Side so he could step all over them.

But the Virgen protected us, and the patrol didn't see.

They threw us out again but, this time, far from the road. From all fronts, people appeared. Hundreds, thousands . . . a grand human river. We joined that caravan. Thousands of peoples joined their dreams with ours. I felt my heart wasn't alone. Little boys, little girls, mothers, fathers, people from all over the world; we all marched firmly forward in hopes of leaving behind our suffering.

I saw the sign that we had arrived: a feathered man flying over metallic trees.

We had finally arrived on the other side!

We are a new tribe: The Migrant Warriors.

We didn't come to fight, we came to search for a piece of happiness. It won't be easy, but the Virgen will keep us safe with her blessing.

I've been brave, and on this journey I've seen many things, terrible and magnificent. But my eyes thirst for tomorrows.

It's the moment to leave our Final Bind to this time. And celebrate the Ceremony of New Fire.

Of a new life.

AUTHOR'S NOTE

When I was looking over the front cover of this book, I heard the tragic news about the death of fifty-three migrants who were hidden inside a trailer heading to Texas.

This codex merely paints a moment in the ever-changing and fleeting story of the brave migrant warriors who search for a better place to live.

This story has continued, continues, and will continue while you hold this book's pages. We are all writers of this story.

Hopefully you, dear reader, contribute to making this earth a bit more humane, a bit more beautiful, a bit more friendly to those unknown guests who will arrive after you.

V.M.

GLOSSARY

Codex: Ancestor to the modern book, where pages are either stacked and fastened to one edge or a single long sheet is secured and then folded up. In both pre-hispanic and colonial times, the Aztecs and Mayans created codices filled with text and art from fig bark (amatl) or other materials.

Tenochtitlán: Modern-day Mexico City and ancient capital of the Aztec Empire, built on Lake Texcoco. According to myth, the city's location was chosen by a prophecy that ordered the Mexica to build a city where they saw a bird perched on a cactus with a snake in its mouth.

Aztecs: Mesoamerican peoples composed of allied tribes that controlled a large part of central México. Though the Aztec Empire was violently overthrown in 1521 by Spanish conquistadores, many Aztec people remain in México today. Also known as the **Triple Alliance**, in reference to the three city-states of Tenochtitlán, Tetzcoco, and Tlacopan.

Mexica: Leading tribe of the Triple Alliance that is commonly known as the Aztec Empire.

Mayans: A diverse, indigenous Mesoamerican people still, largely, found in southern México, El Salvador, Belize, and Honduras. In pre-hispanic times, the Mayans were known for their advanced astronomical and mathematical knowledge.

Iztapalapa: Borough of Mexico City that was formerly an Aztec city of the same name. In pre-hispanic times, Aztecs would go to the city to light the first ceremonial New Fire of their fifty-two-year calendar upon a hill known today as Cerro de la Estrella.

Virgen de Guadalupe: Known as Our Lady of Guadalupe in En-